Stick

The Very Hungry Caterpillar's
EASTER
Sticker & Colouring Book

Your adventure
starts here!
Can you find a sticker of

The Very Hungry
Caterpillar™

to stick on this flower?

This book belongs to

....

PUFFIN

T0354091

1

Let's Go Egg Hunting

There are five Easter eggs hidden around the garden.
When you find an egg, put the matching sticker
in the Easter basket until you have all five!

Stick

Colour

Bunny Hop

Bunnies love Easter! Find a sticker of the sun to put in the sky and then use your favourite colours to colour in these bunnies.

Time to Grow!

**Sunshine helps plants and flowers to grow.
Can you colour in the sun and trees and
use your stickers to fill the field with flowers?**

Stick

Colour

Sunshine and Showers

Weather changes a lot in the springtime. Sometimes it's sunny and sometimes it rains.

Can you find these stickers and complete this sun?

Page 1

Page 2–3 – Let's Go Egg Hunting

Page 4–5 – Bunny Hop

Page 6–7 – Time to Grow!

Page 8 – Sunshine and Showers

Page 10–11 – A Chick's Life Story

Page 10–11 – A Chick's Life Story (continued)

Page 12–13 – Easter Lambs

Page 14–15 – Decorate an Egg

Page 14–15 – Decorate an Egg (continued)

Page 16 – Trees in Bloom

I have completed
The Very Hungry
Caterpillar's
EASTER
Adventure

I have completed
The Very Hungry
Caterpillar's
EASTER
Adventure

Can you join the dots to finish the umbrella? Then use your favourite colours to colour in this scene.

colour me in!

A Chick's Life Story

Baby chicks hatch from eggs. Can you colour in the chicken and find the missing sticker shapes to finish the story?

Stick

Colour

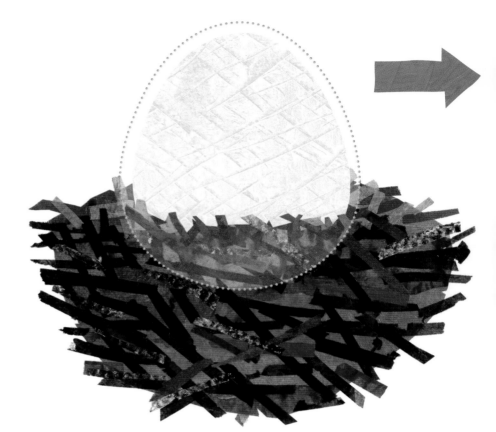

start here

1

A little
egg
sits in
the nest.

5

The chicken
lays another
egg and
the story
begins again.

2

Then a **chick** hatches from the egg.

cheep! cheep!

3

The chick grows up . . .

4

. . . and becomes a **chicken**

colour me in!

11

Easter Lambs

Baby sheep are called lambs. They are born in springtime and play in the fields. Can you use your stickers to fill this field with bouncy lambs?

Stick

12

Stick

Colour

Decorate an Egg

What a big egg! It's a good thing it's for The Very Hungry Caterpillar! Use your favourite colours and stickers to decorate it for him.

Trees in Bloom

Can you use your stickers to cover this tree with flowers? Next, can you add stickers of the animals who call this tree their home?

I have completed
The Very Hungry
Caterpillar's
EASTER
Adventure

Well done!

Can you find your very special stickers? You can stick one here and wear the other one with pride!